The Story of Moses

Written by Sasha Morton
Illustrated by Cherie Zamazing

A long time ago in Egypt, a princess found an Israelite baby floating in a basket beside the riverbank near her palace.

His mother had hidden him away because the pharaoh wanted all Israelite baby boys to be killed.

The pharaoh's kindly daughter adopted the baby and called him Moses, and so an Israelite boy grew up as a member of the Egyptian royal family.

But one day, Moses learned who he really was and became angry about how his people were treated.

Moses fled from the wicked pharaoh. He wandered alone in the desert for many years, married a woman, and had a child. One day, he saw the strangest sight. A bush was on fire, and a voice from within the flames was saying, "Moses, you must free the Israelites!"

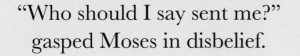

"Who should I say sent me?"
gasped Moses in disbelief.

"I AM who I AM," boomed the voice of
God. "And with my help, you will lead the
pharaoh's slaves out of Egypt, to a land
where they can live in freedom."

"Ask the pharaoh to release his slaves. He will not listen, but you should drop your staff to the floor. It will turn into a snake and then he may believe that I have sent you," said God.

As God had predicted, the pharaoh refused to listen to Moses.
He wasn't even persuaded by the staff turning into a snake!
So God sent another message…

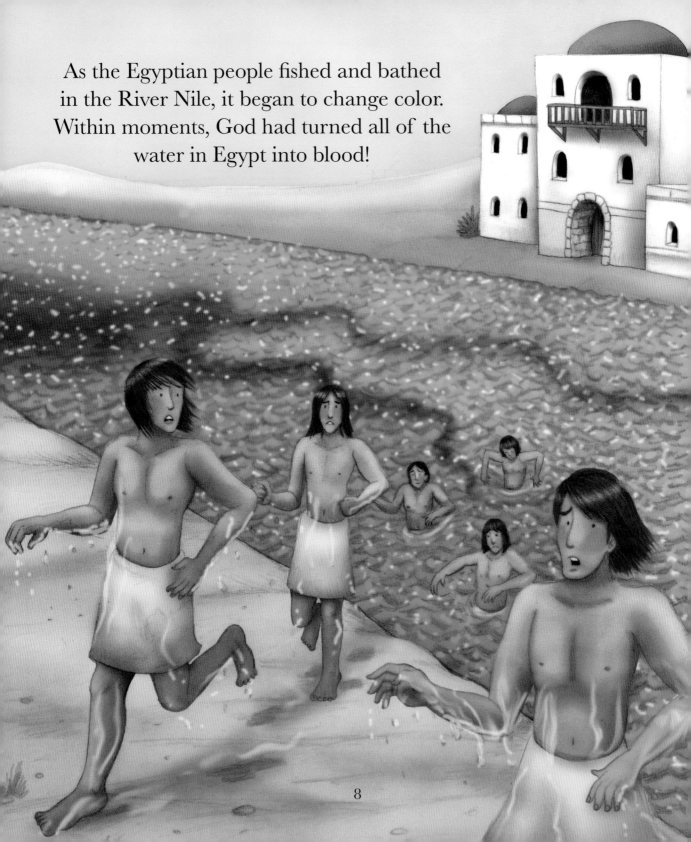

As the Egyptian people fished and bathed
in the River Nile, it began to change color.
Within moments, God had turned all of the
water in Egypt into blood!

8

There was no clean water to wash in or to drink. But worse was soon to come.

For every day that the pharaoh refused to free the Israelites, God sent a terrible plague into Egypt.

9

Frogs rained down,
    mosquitoes bit everyone,
        and flies made all the Egyptians itch.

Their cattle died,

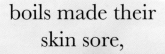

boils made their
skin sore,

and hailstones, heavy
enough to shatter trees,
fell from the skies.

By now, every Egyptian wanted
the pharaoh to set his slaves free,
but the pharaoh refused.

11

So God sent a cloud of locusts.
He plunged the land into darkness and
then he sent the worst plague of all…

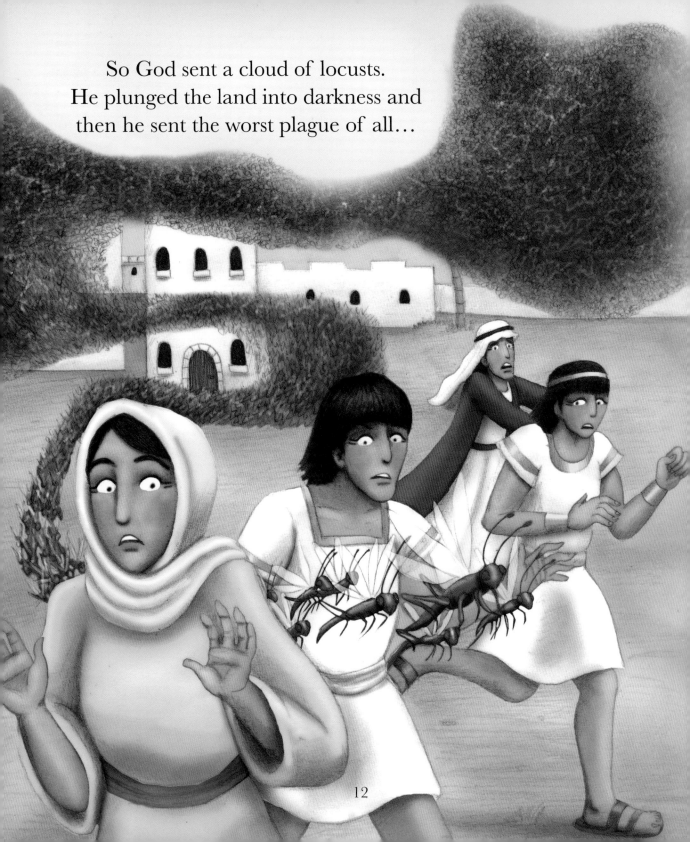

Every firstborn Egyptian child died,
including the pharaoh's own son.

At last, the pharaoh gave in.
Moses could lead the Israelites
to God's Promised Land.

They were free at last!

God sent a pillar of cloud by day and a pillar of fire by night to guide Moses and his people through the desert.

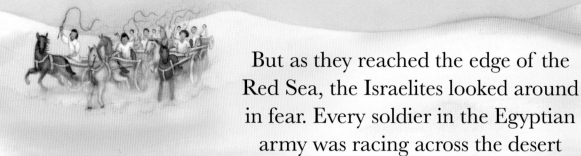

But as they reached the edge of the
Red Sea, the Israelites looked around
in fear. Every soldier in the Egyptian
army was racing across the desert
to capture them!

The pharaoh had changed his mind.
Who would build and clean his palaces?
He needed those slaves back!

Moses' people were in despair, and
some even thought they should go back
to the pharaoh. They were trapped,
with the Red Sea before them and six
hundred chariots behind them!

But God had told Moses what to do.

"Have no fear," said Moses, as he lifted his rod and stretched his hand out over the sea. To everyone's astonishment, the waves drew back to make two walls of water. Before them was a dry path that would lead the Israelites to freedom at last!

Quickly, the Israelites fled through the tunnel
of water. The Egyptian army tried to follow them,
but God's pillar of cloud swirled around the
soldiers, confusing them.

Once Moses' people had safely crossed the Red Sea,
God lifted the cloud and the army charged after them.

As soon as every chariot was on the path, Moses raised his hand
again. The two huge walls of water tumbled back together, and
within moments, the entire army was washed away!

How the Israelites cheered!
Together, they joined Moses in prayer
and thanked God for their freedom.

Moses led the Israelites through the wilderness for three long months. At last, God sent for Moses to come to the top of a mountain so he could speak with him.

While a fire burned brightly at the top of Mount Sinai, Moses' people waited for their leader to return to them.

Moses was up on the mountain for forty days and forty nights.
When he returned, he brought a gift from God. Written on two
stone tablets by the Lord himself were ten special laws that
God wanted his people to live by.

And carrying these Commandments
with them, the people who once
were slaves set off to live in freedom,
just as God himself had promised.

An Hachette UK Company
www.hachette.co.uk

First published in the USA in 2014 by Ticktock,
an imprint of Octopus Publishing Group Ltd
Endeavour House
189 Shaftesbury Avenue
London
WC2H 8JY
www.octopusbooks.co.uk
www.octopusbooksusa.com
www.ticktockbooks.com

Distributed in the US by
Hachette Book Group USA
237 Park Avenue
New York, NY 10017, USA

Distributed in Canada by
Canadian Manda Group
165 Dufferin Street
Toronto, Ontario, Canada M6K 3H6

ISBN 978 1 84898 830 9

Printed and bound in China

10 9 8 7 6 5 4 3 2 1

With thanks to Jana Burson

Series Editor: Lucy Cuthew US Editor: Jennifer Dixon
Design: Advocate Art Publisher: Tim Cook
Managing Editor: Karen Rigden
Production Controller: Sarah-Jayne Johnson